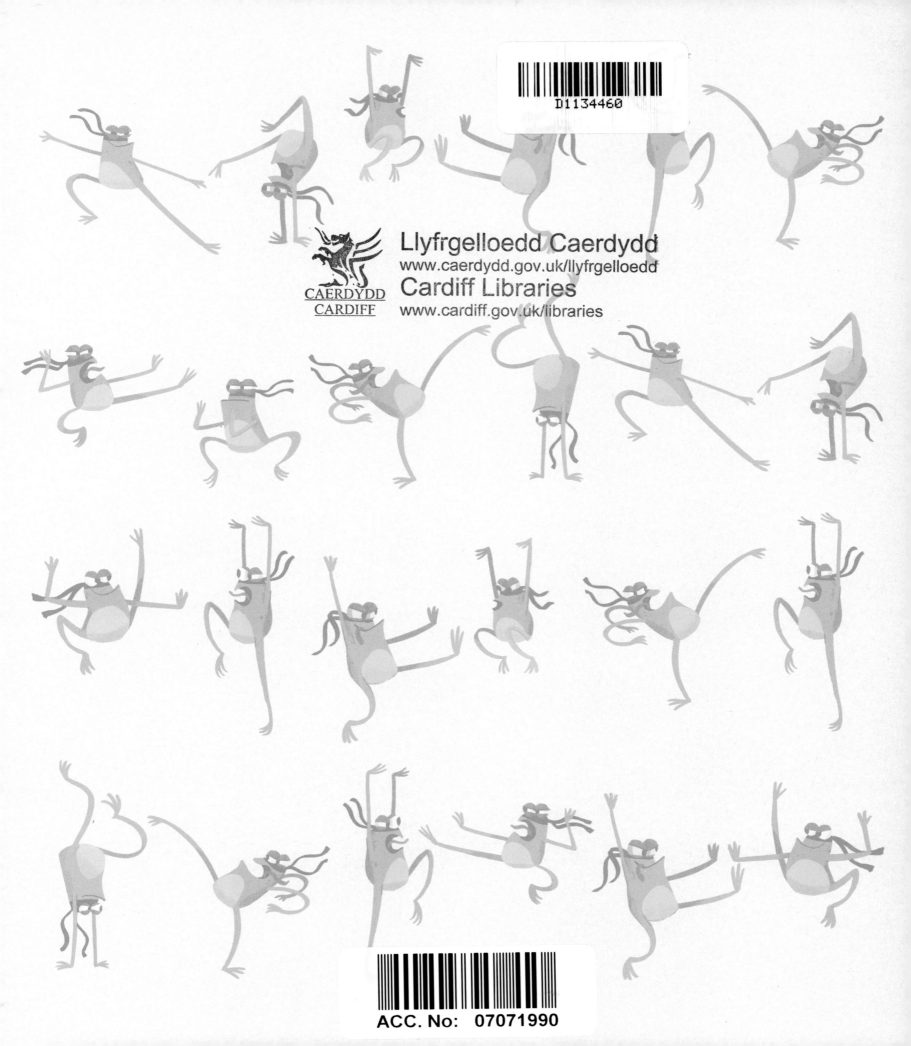

# The Tale of the Valiant Ninja Frog

For Pieter and Janneke ~ A.C.

For Ian and Glenys ~ J.T.

**WALKER BOOKS**
AND SUBSIDIARIES
LONDON • BOSTON • SYDNEY • AUCKLAND

First published 2020 by Walker Books Ltd, 87 Vauxhall Walk, London SE11 5HJ • Text © 2020 Alastair Chisholm • Illustrations © 2020 Jez Tuya • The right of Alastair Chisholm and Jez Tuya to be identified as author and illustrator respectively of this work has been asserted by them in accordance with the Copyright, Designs and Patents Act 1988 • This book has been typeset in Futura T Medium and ITC New Baskerville • Printed in China • All rights reserved. No part of this book may be reproduced transmitted or stored in an information retrieval system in any form or by any means, graphic, electronic or mechanical, including photocopying, taping and recording without prior written permission from the publisher • British Library Cataloguing in Publication Data: a catalogue record for this book is available from the British Library
ISBN 9781406388640 • www.walker.co.uk • 10 9 8 7 6 5 4 3 2 1

# The Tale of the Valiant Ninja Frog

Alastair Chisholm

illustrated by Jez Tuya

The stars twinkled, the moon shone,
and Dad, Jamie and Abby sat by a campfire,
cooking marshmallows.

"Tell us a story, Dad!" said Jamie.
"Yes, a story!" said Abby.
"What kind of story?" asked Dad.
"One with the Prince," said Jamie.
"And the Frog," said Abby.
"And the Princess, and the Witch!" said Jamie.
"Don't forget the Frog," said Abby.
"And ..." said Jamie, "a MONSTER."
"Right," said Dad. "Ready?"

"IT WAS A DARK AND STORMY NIGHT," said Dad,
"and at the bottom of a horrible mountain,
in the shadow of a horrible castle,
deep within a horrible forest …
were the *heroes*.

"There was the Prince and his horse – handsome, brave and bold!

"There was the Princess – cunning, beautiful, and secretly known as Fingers Malloy, daredevil jewel thief!

"And there was Bogwort the Witch!
Magical, mysterious, and occasionally ... a *Ninja*."

"What about the Frog?" asked Abby.
"Oh yes," said Dad.
"There was also the Witch's tiny frog, just as big as your thumb, who she kept tucked away nice and safe."

"He's always being kept safe," complained Abby.
"Can't he be a hero too?"
"He's too small," said Jamie.
"But he's very brave!"
"Too small!" said Jamie.
"Hmmph," said Abby.

"Our heroes," said Dad,
"were there because of a dreadful ogre named ...
GRUBBER THE GRUESOME.
Grubber the Gruesome was *enormous*.

"He had warts
the size of plates…

"His hands were
as big as tables…

"And the breath from
his vast mouth carried
the awful stench …
of *broccoli*."
"Yuck!" said Jamie.
"I *like* broccoli," said Abby.

"He was a rotten meanie," said Dad,
"and he'd stolen all the keys to the kingdom.
Without their keys, no one could do anything.
They couldn't get into their homes!
They couldn't start their horses!
It was *chaos*."

"Like the time I accidentally dropped your
keys down the drain?" asked Jamie.
"Yes," said Dad. "Exactly like that."

"Grubber had hidden the keys in a deep dungeon
in his home, Castle Normus.
But our heroes had a cunning plan.

"That evening, as Grubber sat in his parlour chuckling to himself about how rotten he was, there was a knock at the door – *knock-knock-knock!*
'Who dares disturb me?'
bellowed the ogre.

"It was the heroes!
'We're circus performers!' they said.
'We're here to entertain you!'

"'Behold,' said the Prince, 'the incredible skills of …
Andrew the Amazing Horse!'
Andrew the Amazing Horse could do all sorts of tricks,
such as … standing on his head.

"And…"

"Juggling!" said Jamie.
"Yes, juggling!" said Dad.

"And walking the tightrope!" said Jamie.
"Sure," said Dad. "Why not?"

"But while Andrew the Amazing Horse distracted the ogre, the Princess and the Witch sneaked past.

"The Witch waved her wicked wand and shook her furtive feet. She hissed a crooked curse and glared an evil eye …

"and turned the dungeon door into *jelly*.

"Then the Princess threw her grappling rope, and leapt! And swung down ... down ... down to the bottom of the dungeon.

"And there they were...
*All the keys to the kingdom.*"

"Wait," said Abby. "What did Barry do?"

"Who's Barry?" asked Dad.

"Barry the Frog! What did he do?"

"Oh…" said Dad. "Um … Barry kept lookout."

"That's *boring*," said Abby.

"Barry never gets to do anything!"

"I told you," said Jamie.

"He's far too small to be important."

"*Hmmph*," muttered Abby again.

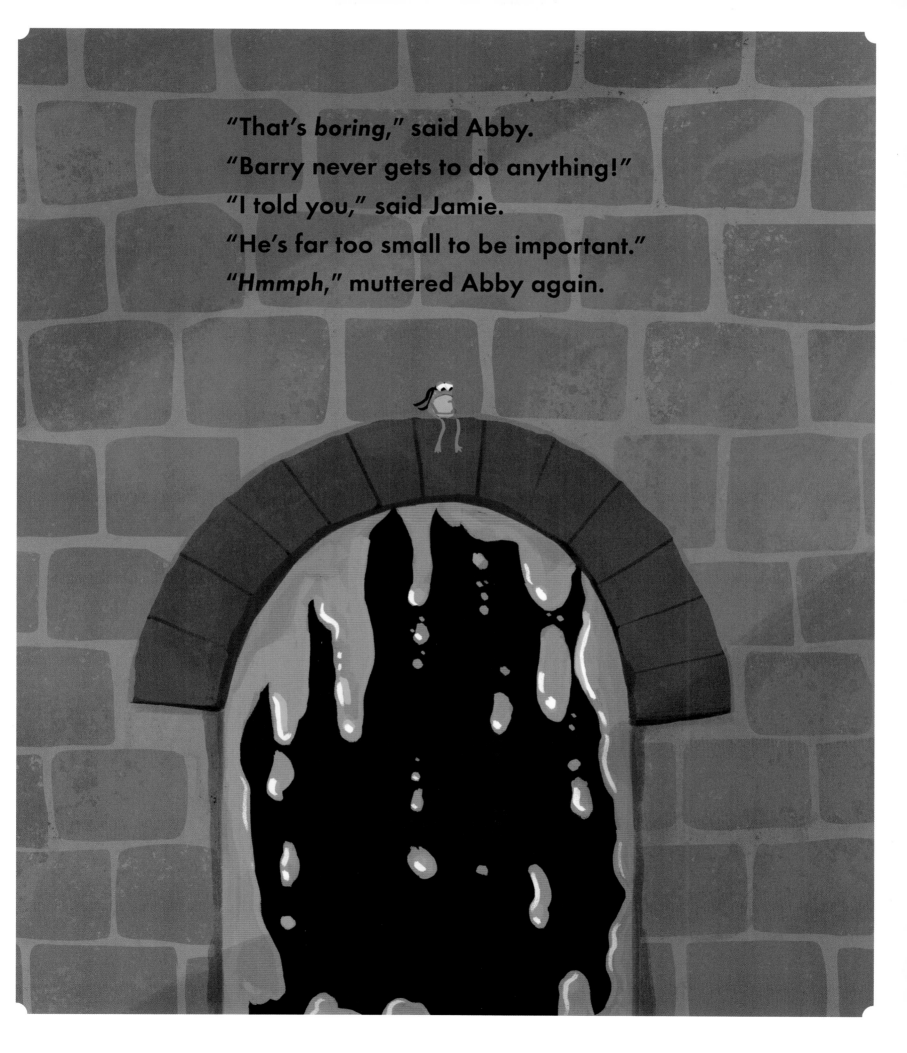

"The Princess scooped up the keys," said Dad,
"and the Witch hauled her back up.
 But then, suddenly—"
"The alarm went off!" shouted Jamie.
 "That's right!" said Dad.
 "A huge clanging bell rang
through the castle!"

"And then Grubber ran after
them and caught them all!"
shouted Jamie.
"He did!" said Dad.
"In his huge, hairy fists!"
"And then," said Jamie,
"Grubber roared...

"Oh, no!" gasped Dad and Abby.

"So how did they escape?" asked Jamie.

"Oh," said Dad. "Um..."

 He stopped. He scratched his head.

*"I don't know."*

"I know—" said Abby.

"Wait, I know!" shouted Jamie. "The Prince fights Grubber!"

"But Grubber's too strong," said Dad.

"I know—" said Abby.

"Maybe the Witch does some magic?" said Jamie.

"But she can't wave her wand to cast a spell," said Dad.

"Stop!" shouted Abby.
*"I KNOW WHAT HAPPENS!"*
"Barry the Valiant Ninja Frog rescues them all!"

"No, no, no," sighed Jamie.
"He can't fight Grubber –
he's far too small!"
*"Exactly!"* said Abby.
"He was so small that he could
*creep between Grubber's fingers.*

"And then Barry,
*who was also a Ninja,*
snuck around Grubber's back,
and then up
onto his head!

"And Grubber stumbled about,
and lost his balance,
and fell over…

"And he dropped the others,
and together they tied him up!

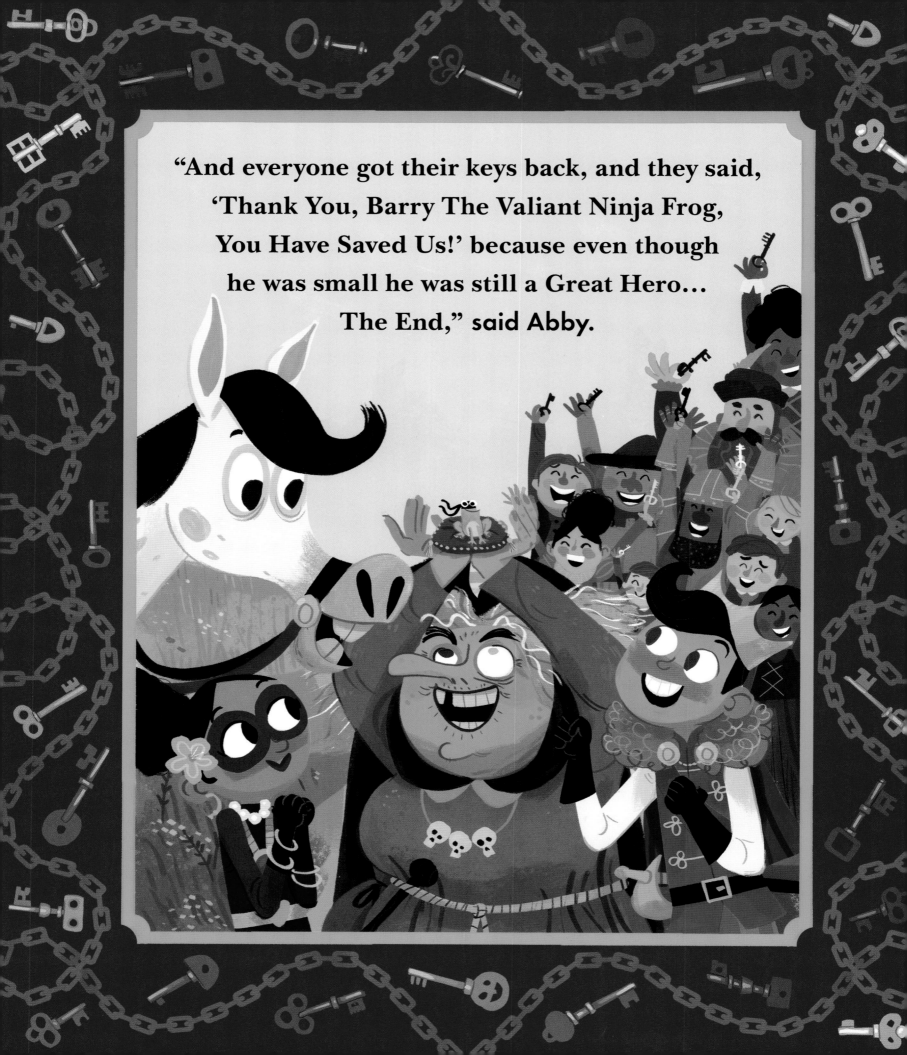

"And everyone got their keys back, and they said, 'Thank You, Barry The Valiant Ninja Frog, You Have Saved Us!' because even though he was small he was still a Great Hero… The End," said Abby.

"Wow," said Jamie. "Good story!"
"Well done, Abby!" said Dad.
"Thank you," said Abby. "Barry did most of it."

The campfire had died down
and it was almost time for bed.
Jamie and Abby snuggled up close to Dad
and gazed at the night sky,
and the twinkling stars above them.
"What story shall we have tomorrow?"
yawned Jamie, sleepily.
"What do you think, Abby?" asked Dad.
Abby looked at the stars. "Hmm," she said.
"I know..."

ᶻᶻᶻᶻᶻᶻᶻᶻᶻᶻ

# "SPACE PIRATE BEARS."

"Of course!" said Dad, and he tucked them
into their camp beds and kissed them goodnight.